Journey Home

BY LAWRENCE MCKAY, JR.

ILLUSTRATED BY DOM & KEUNHEE LEE

LEE & LOW BOOKS, INC. · NEW YORK

For Susan,
the music in my life

I'd like to acknowledge Annie Allen for her generosity and
friendship, and Liz Szabla at Lee & Low for her astute advice —L.M.

To the people who have two homelands —D. & K.L.

Text copyright © 1998 by Lawrence McKay, Jr.
Illustrations copyright © 1998 by Dom and Keunhee Lee
All rights reserved. No part of the contents of this book may be reproduced by
any means without the written permission of the publisher.
LEE & LOW BOOKS Inc., 95 Madison Avenue, New York, NY 10016
leeandlow.com

Manufactured in China by South China Printing Co.

Book design by Tania Garcia
Book production by The Kids at Our House

Editorial and Language Consultant:
Cindy Le, Heinle & Heinle, ITP, Delray Beach, FL

The text is set in 14 pt. Sabon
The illustrations are rendered by applying encaustic beeswax on paper, then
scratching out images, and finally adding oil paint and colored pencil.

Author's Note: For the sake of pronunciation and ease of reading I have
purposely chosen to use the Chinese appellation of "Kuan Yin," the
Goddess of Mercy. Even though *Journey Home* is set in Vietnam, the
Vietnamese appellation would have introduced prohibitive typesetting
issues to the manufacture of this English-language book.

(HC) 10 9 8 7 6 5 4 3 2 1
(PB) 10 9 8 7 6 5 4 3
First Edition

Library of Congress Cataloging-in-Publication Data
McKay, Lawrence.
Journey home/by Lawrence McKay, Jr;
illustrated by Dom and Keunhee Lee.—1st ed.
p.   cm.
Summary: Mai returns to Vietnam, the land of her mother's birth,
to discover both a new country and something about herself.
ISBN 1-880000-65-2 (hardcover)   ISBN 1-58430-005-1 (paperback)
[1. Vietnam—Fiction. 2. Vietnamese Americans—Fiction.]
I. Lee, Dom, ill. II. Lee, Keunhee, ill. III. Title.
PZ7.M4786575Jo   1998
[Fic]—dc21   97-31407

Mom and I are packing for our big trip to Vietnam. A long time ago when Mom was a baby she was left at an orphanage in Saigon during the Vietnam War. The nuns named her Trinh Nu Linh, but these days Mom is called Lin. Now, Mom's going back and taking me with her to help search for her birth family. I'm excited, but I'm also afraid of what we'll find when we get there.

I want to take the kite on my wall, but Mom says it's too fragile to make the journey. The kite was her only possession when she was adopted and brought to America. Mom doesn't know where the kite came from. Her past is like a puzzle. The kite is one of the pieces that still doesn't fit.

Ever since we decided to go to Vietnam, Mom and I have been reading more about the country, the Buddha, and Kuan Yin. I've always liked the stories about Kuan Yin the best. She's the Goddess of Mercy. "At the cry of misery, Kuan Yin hears the voice, then removes the sorrow," Mom says. I hope Kuan Yin hears Mom's wish, and helps us find our other family.

Last week, I celebrated my tenth birthday. All my friends came to my party. Mom's adoptive father was there, too, my grandfather. Mom is a research scientist for a big company just like he once was. I think Mom takes after him. I'm lucky because I love my family and they love me.

Two years ago, when my grandmother died, Mom began to think about going to Vietnam to find her birth family. She spent a lot of time at night researching and writing letters. At first she thought she should go alone. But I told her I was old enough to go and help her find our other family.

Mom and I are flying in a 747 high over the Pacific. I look out the window and take a deep breath. What if Mom's other parents are dead? I try to put that thought out of my head, but it keeps coming back. Sometimes, I think Mom's crazy. She doesn't even know where they live, or their name, or even if they're alive.

I don't know how she can be so calm. I glance at Mom as she studies her Vietnamese phrase book. This year, she's been taking lessons in Vietnamese. The language seemed strange to me at first, but Mom has taught me a few words. I like the sound of it on my tongue.

"If we find them will we stay in Vietnam?" I ask.

Mom smiles, takes my hand, and squeezes. "No, our home is in America." I hope so. Gazing out at the ocean, I wonder what my friends are doing today.

We land in Saigon, and the first things I see are palm trees, jungle, and the hazy outlines of the city. "Wouldn't it be great if your family could be here to meet us," I say, trying to be cheerful. But Mom doesn't answer. I can tell she is nervous. It's scary when you don't know what's ahead of you.

Our hotel room looks like the one we stayed in when we went to New York last year to see a play. Looking outside at the buildings and the crowds of people, I try to imagine what it was like during the war, but it's hard to believe there ever was a war here.

Today we're going to check the birth records. While Mom gets dressed I look at myself in the mirror. It's strange being in a country where I look mostly like everyone else. I'm used to being a little different, like the way I am back home.

After Mom gets directions to the People's Hall of Records where the birth records are kept, we set out. We take a bike-taxi called a cyclo. Thousands of people surround us, riding their bikes between cars, trucks, and buses. The air is hot and smells like exhaust. I try to act as brave as Mom.

Inside the People's Hall of Records, Mom shows a clerk a photograph. I love that picture because it shows Mom in the orphanage when she was two years old, holding the same kite that hangs on my wall. We spend the day looking at books filled with pictures, trying to find a match of Mom, but nothing turns up. The clerk shakes his head sadly, sorry he can't be of more help.

I know how Mom feels, because I've never seen my father either. His name was Frank Mercer and he left before I was born. Mom doesn't know where he is, and he's never tried to find me. I don't understand why people can't stay together.

The next day, a driver takes us to the countryside. "Stop!" Mom says, pointing to a statue near the road. "There's Kuan Yin."

We get out of the car and stand in front of Kuan Yin. I think about my life and how lucky I am. Mom's lucky too, to have made it to America and a good family. "Please help Mom," I whisper, staring up into Kuan Yin's eyes.

Back in Saigon, we visit orphanages, walking door to door, showing Mom's picture to the nuns. Inside are hundreds of photographs of lost children tacked to the walls. I don't even want to think about how it would feel to be lost from Mom. Is this how she has always felt? Lost?

I know Mom is feeling down because we haven't turned up anything yet. I feel like giving up. Mom senses this and says, "All we can do is keep trying."

We take a taxi to a market near the waterfront. We walk past stalls where the merchants and farmers sell their wares. Some even speak English. Mom buys me a ring. Then, near the pier, I see a stall with kites.

Mom points to a kite and my heart jumps. It looks a lot like the kite on my wall at home. Mom asks the merchant about it, but he doesn't speak English. She shows him her photograph. He grins and points to the picture, then the kite. Mom pulls out her phrase book, but in her excitement, she can't find the right words. The merchant writes something on a piece of paper and hands it to her. Back at the hotel, a man at the desk translates it for us. It is a place, he says, called Sa Dec, and a name: Tran Quang Tai.

We hire another driver and travel south toward the city of Sa Dec. Sometimes, we stop in the middle of the road, because farmers with carts pulled by oxen block our way. It looks much poorer here in the countryside, but it seems peaceful, too.

"Was the war here too?" I ask, hoping to see ruins or bomb craters. "Yes," the driver replies, "but nature soon takes over everything and you have to look hard to see the scars."

I try to imagine what it would be like to hear bombs exploding all around me. Did someone help Mom escape down this road?

At an outdoor market in Sa Dec, Mom shows her picture to the merchants and asks about Tran Quang Tai. Finally, a woman selling jewelry tells us in English that Tran Quang Tai is absent today. She gives us directions to his village a few miles away.

We come to the village and get out of the car. The air is heavy and wet. I see a few small children playing in the dirt and hear a dog barking. A pathway leads to a clearing with a few small houses. When the driver stops a boy and asks directions to the kite maker's place, the boy smiles and points to the second house.

Mom and I stand at the doorway. My heart pounds. Inside we see an old man and a girl my age. "Hello," Mom says slowly, "I am looking for Tran Quang Tai." The girl stares at me. I try to smile.

Mom shows him the picture. As he gazes at it a tear trickles down his cheek. He looks up and searches Mom's eyes with his own, and then touches her hand with his bony fingers.

He motions to the girl and says something in Vietnamese. After a moment, she translates.

"My grandfather cannot speak your language, and for this, he asks your apology." Mom pulls out her phrase book, but the old man holds up his hand. The girl continues, "I am Tran Quang Tai, the kite maker, but the man who made your kite, and taught me this art, was your father." Tran Quang Tai hesitates, then he and the girl continue.

"Your father died in the bombing with your mother. I was his student and friend. When our village was destroyed, I found you in the rubble under the kite your father made for you. After I repaired it, I carried you and the kite to Saigon and placed you on the steps of an orphanage. I feared that if I went inside, the nuns would believe that I was your father and turn you away. I wanted to raise you as a daughter, but it was too dangerous. I didn't even know if I would live out the day. Behind the orphanage walls I knew you'd be safe. When the war ended I asked about you, but the orphanage was gone."

Tran Quang Tai takes Mom's hands. "You are Le Duc Lan."

There are tears on Mom's cheeks. It is the first time I've ever seen her cry.

"Is this home?" I ask. Mom takes a breath, wipes her eyes, and finally answers, "Inside me, yes, because here I was born. But the world changes, Mai, and even though I lived through that change, I have been away too long." Mom pulls me to her. "I've found what I thought I'd never find, my name, and for that I'll never again feel the emptiness of not knowing. That can never be taken away from me."

Where is home, I wonder. Is it inside me, like Mom says, or all around me? I was born in America and my name is Mai. Yet when I look into Tran Quang Tai's eyes, I feel like I belong here, too. I think home must be inside me and all around me too.

We all walk up the hill to the pagoda where Mom's mother and father's ashes are kept with thousands of others, all mixed together. Mom and I stand in front of the shrine to Kuan Yin. Mom holds the old photograph up to her heart and bows her head.

I touch Kuan Yin and whisper, "Thank you."